Jack's Room

■SCHOLASTIC

Children's Press®
A Division of Scholastic Inc.
New York Toronto London Auckland Sydney Mexico City
New Delhi Hong Kong Danbury, Connecticut

Early Childhood Consultants:

Ellen Booth Church
Diane Ohanesian

SCHOLASTIC, CHILDREN'S PRESS, ROOKIE PRESCHOOL, and associated logos are trademarks and/or registered trademarks of Scholastic Inc.

1 2 3 4 5 6 7 8 9 10 R 19 18 17 16 15 14 13 12 11 10   62

Library of Congress Cataloging-in-Publication Data

Woolf, Julia.
 Jack's room / Julia Woolf.
   p. cm. — (Rookie preschool)
 Summary: A cumulative rhyme describes the contents of the room in which young Jack is preparing for bed.
   ISBN-13: 978-0-531-24400-5 (lib. bdg.)   ISBN-13: 978-0-531-24575-0 (pbk.)
   ISBN-10: 0-531-24400-8 (lib. bdg.)   ISBN-10: 0-531-24575-6 (pbk.)

 1. Stories in rhyme. 2. Bedrooms—Fiction. 3. Bedtime—Fiction. 4. African Americans—Fiction. I. Title. II. Series.
PZA.3.W8935Jac 2009
 [E] – dc22   2009004774

This is Jack.

This is the room where Jack sleeps.

This is the bed
so comfy and red,

that stands in the room where Jack sleeps.

Point to the bear
so fuzzy and fair,

that sits by the bed
so comfy and red,

that stands in the room where Jack sleeps.

Do you see the jeep
that goes beep-beep,

that holds the bear
so fuzzy and fair,

that sits by the bed
so comfy and red,

that stands in the room where Jack sleeps?

Look for the clock
that goes tick tock,

that's near the jeep
that goes beep-beep,

that holds the bear
so fuzzy and fair,

that sits by the bed
so comfy and red,

that stands in the room where Jack sleeps.

Find the book at which Jack will look,

that rests by the clock
that goes tick tock,

that's near the jeep
that goes beep-beep,

that holds the bear
so fuzzy and fair,

that sits by the bed
so comfy and red,

that stands in the room where Jack sleeps.

Where is the light that's turned low at night,

that shines on the book
at which Jack will look,

that rests by the clock
that goes tick tock,

that's near the jeep
that goes beep-beep,

that holds the bear
so fuzzy and fair,

that sits by the bed
so comfy and red,

that stands in the room where Jack sleeps?

18

This is the hug
so cozy and snug,

that Mom gives to Jack,
and Jack gives right back.

19

Now . . .

It's time to turn off the light,
that shines on the book,

that rests by the clock,

that's near the jeep,

that held the bear,

that's now in the bed
so comfy and red,

that stands in the room where Jack sleeps.

Good night, Jack.

Rookie Storytime Tips

In this new version of a classic nursery rhyme, Jack's Room explores the familiar objects in a young child's room as he goes through his bedtime routine. When you share this book with your preschooler, invite him or her to fill in some of the rhyming words as the poem progresses. It's a playful way to build an understanding of rhyme, a key pre-literacy skill.

Invite your child to go back through the book and find the following:

A TOY CAR and all the other things that go

A CIRCLE on the wall and all the other circles in Jack's room

A GREEN MONSTER and all the other things that are green

Along the way, you will reinforce classification, and color and shape recognition, more skills in the preschool curriculum.

Play a rhyming game! Ask your child to think of words that rhyme with: Jack, bear, bed, and clock. How many can he or she think of?